Jellybean Books™

The Bunny Ball

By Annie Ingle
Illustrated by Katy Bratun

For my son, Eric, with all my love
—K.B.

Random House 🏠 New York

Text copyright © 1994 by Random House, Inc. Illustrations copyright © 1994 by Katy Bratun. All rights reserved.
Originally published in different form in 1994 as a Random House Pictureback® Book. First Random House
Jellybean Books™ edition, 1999. Library of Congress Catalog Card Number: 98–65562
ISBN 0-679-89258-3 (trade) ; 0-679-99258-8 (lib. bdg.)
www.randomhouse.com/kids/
Printed in the United States of America 10 9 8 7 6 5 4 3 2 1

JELLYBEAN BOOKS is a trademark of Random House, Inc.

When the moon is full
and the air is sweet
and the crickets
begin to thrum…

and fireflies flicker
and raccoons bicker
and the bullfrog
beats soft his drum…

slip on your sweater
and sneak to the woods
and crouch in the dark
on your knees.

You might just see
a wondrous sight
that only the
lucky ones see.

It's the Bunnies' Ball!
A splendid dance,
and all good bunnies
are there—

cottontail, jackrabbit,
lop-ear,
and, of course,
the Belgian hare.

Chipmunks fix
a sumptuous feast
of dew and
dandelion punch,
of crackers smeared
with carrot cream,
of watercress quiche
to munch.

There are tortes and tarts
and turnip tops and ices to
last the night.
For chipmunks know
it is their job
to get each
detail right.

The musicians come
a little late—
but better late
than never.
For far and wide
these minstrels are known
as the greatest
dance band ever.

Three tree frogs,
a cricket quartet,
a beaver who
plays his tail.
Two wild dogs,
a shrill katydid,
and a soulful
nightingale.

The trumpets blare,
and doors swing wide.
The bunnies
two by two
emerge in moonlight,
blinking, preening,
sashaying
into view.

O elegant bunnies!
They waltz and whirl
in finery and pomp.
Then the band
picks up the beat
and the bunnies
start to stomp.
They romp, they kick,
they rock, they roll,
they shake loose leaves
from the trees.
In all your life
you've never seen
such revelers as these!

So now you've
seen the
wondrous sight
that only the lucky
ones see.
It's time to come
out of the bushes
and dust off
both your knees.

Go on home,
you've had enough,
you've surely
had your fill

of berry tarts
and carrot cream
and tasty treats,
until…

the moon is full
and the air is sweet
and the crickets
begin to thrum
and fireflies flicker
and raccoons bicker
and the bullfrog
beats soft his drum.